For the readers who love a swinging good time. This one's for you.

And...for *Fredrico*.

Chapter One

A vast body of greenish-blue water stretched as far as the eye could see. Waves breeched the pristine shoreline of the only home Tarzan had ever known. In the dense jungle behind him, primary huffs from family members filled the air with a deep organic sound.

As the surf crashed onto the beach in a mighty show of power, another high-pitched scream cut through the froth of angry waves.

Closer this time.

Tarzan deepened his crouch behind the abundant leaves used to line his moon-bed. Curling a finger around a thick stalk, he pushed it lower to study the shore. A blue object floated in the ebb and flow, caught in the sharp barnacles at low tide. The color of the sky thrashed in the water, crying out in pitiful mews.

He again scanned the horizon for ships that occasionally ventured too close to his island home. The endless line where water met sky appeared as ordinary as the struggling object was out of place.

A grunt from behind, followed by a gentle bump to his shoulder, warned him to stay wary.

"*Ooh-ooh*," he grunted in reply, then turned and looked into the worried eyes of Echo, his ape brother. Tarzan lifted his chin to point at a tall tree, where the bark peeled in long, hanging strips. "*Ooh-ooh.*"

Echo gave a hard stare, then swiftly crossed the short distance to swing up into higher branches using his powerful arms.

After a final sweep of the beach and sea, Tarzan carefully stepped out from the protection of his beloved jungle and onto the warm, soft sand. With silent footfalls, he crept closer to the unknown object. Two arms flailed weakly in the surge, and the larger body of water pulled back as another curl formed.

"Help me! Oh my God, help—" Tones of the frantic voice disappeared in the ceaseless onslaught that battered the island.

Human!

Startled, Tarzan straightened from his crouched stance. He moved closer, watching the human's small hands grab for the flesh-tearing, barnacle-covered rocks. Long hair, the color of the mineral-rich mud bordering the pools below the waterfall, flattened against a small skull that reared up, out of the tide. He couldn't see the human's face through all the hair, but he heard the unmistakable gasp rent the air.

Before the next surge pushed forward to cover the human's head, he made a quick decision to help the weakling, who floundered like a newborn gorilla caught in the drag of the sea.

Less than two leaps away, a sharp-pointed fin broke the water's surface. Drawn by the smell of blood, more would appear in a matter of time.

The stranger lifted a hand out of the water, weaker now, vainly reaching for a source to save him. The arm bore a reddish skin cover sprinkled with tiny yellow flowers that ended below the crook of a delicately boned arm. Colored rocks circled the wrist, and a shiny type of silver metal circled the middle finger.

The fin turned with a splash from the meat-eater's tail. If the human were to survive, Tarzan had to act now.

Avoiding the human's injured palm, he grasped the small wrist and hoped the bones beneath his tight grip wouldn't break. Instead of pulling the limp body up, out of the surf, he waited for the next wave to lift the dead weight. Carefully stepping horizontally across the rock and sharp barnacles, he moved away from the dangerous part of the shore. Only when the soles of his feet touched coarse pebbles of shallow water did he move backward to where the sand lay warm and dry.

Safe from the fish that tore meat from the bone, he dropped the thin arm lacking the necessary muscle to survive. He stepped back a few paces and crouched on his haunches to watch. Stomach-side down, the small human lay still for so long he feared he'd been too late.

Two thin legs, covered in dark blue to the knees, jerked and twitched. One cough, then another, followed mouthfuls of regurgitated water and a long string of more hacking coughs. The weakling's arms moved under his chest and pushed at the sand. Turning to flop onto his back, the person lay there taking in great gulps of air and coughing out droplets of sea water. Sand covered a portion of a child-like face; the rest of the features were covered by wet, matted hair.

From his huddled position, Tarzan scanned the beach before crab-walking closer to investigate. Curious, he reached his finger forward and slid a hunk of wet hair off the small, pale face.

S altwater tore a burning path up her raw throat as Jane coughed and took in another lungful of delicious air.

"My God." No amount of lozenges could help at this point. Maybe a shot—or five—of the hundred-year-old brandy in her desk drawer at home would do the trick.

No, she'd be better off pouring the stuff over her shredded hand to kill the germs.

Warm sand under her back, hot sun on her face. If the nightmare of the sinking yacht weren't fresh and foremost in her mind, she could have been at any number of tropical resorts. Damn the pirate crew for leaving her behind, even if she'd been held against her will. Whether or not they were really pirates or a band of human traffickers, her value as a human was worth more than live bait for fish.

She'd been jarred awake from shouts and the drum of running feet above deck before a dark-skinned man, hardly older than herself, burst into her stateroom and ordered her out at gunpoint. After she'd been shoved overboard, she had no idea what had happened to the evil crew.

As if in a dream, she slowly became aware of a soft stroking at her cheek. Tired...Lord, she was tired.

"*Ooh.*"

What the hell was that? A grunt?

"*Ooh-ooh.*"

Fingers, definitely fingers, pushed hard against her cheek, rolling her head side to side. She wanted to tell the asshole to quit poking at her. As soon as she spat out all the sand crunching between her teeth, she'd get right on it.

The finger-poke moved lower into personal space territory. If her nipples beaded in response, then oh well.

A warm, rough palm gently squeezed her left breast. Jane pried her eyes open and blinked away loose sand.

A fully bearded man peered down. Curious brown eyes studied her face, then shifted to where his hand tightened over her breast. His dark-blond hair lay in knots twisted so tight, it would've sent her stylist screaming from the salon.

He searched her eyes again, searching for what, she couldn't say. His hand slid off her boob and skated further south, heading for the same paradise all men pursued. Had she escaped being kidnapped only to find herself possibly raped?

When his palm reached her belly button with no signs of slowing, the free-for-all grope fest was officially over.

"Hey! Knock it off." She moved to bat his hand away, but only flicked him on the end of his nose instead. Her hand fell back to the sand.

Well, at least I tried, she thought.

"*Uh-uh.*"

Great, more grunting.

Chapter Two

Judging by her testy mood, the human female appeared unharmed. Her breasts were smaller than the females in Tarzan's family, though he appreciated her lack of body hair. She'd objected to his familiarization of her human's form. If she were scared, that could be a reason she'd hit him on the nose.

He backed off two steps, then waited in his crouch to see what she'd do next. Even bad-tempered, the tone of her voice soothed his ears, and he wondered if he touched her again, would she make more of the same?

The melody of her mouth-sounds warbled in pitch as though she sang in appreciation of the beautiful day. She repeated the song, staring at him with expectation in the arch of her lowered brows.

A fistful of sand thrown his direction wasn't what he expected. Tarzan scratched the hair on his chin, the only similarity shared with his ape family. The female's striking blue eyes snared him in a hypnotic web he didn't wish to escape.

Her mouth-noise rose in volume as she struggled to sit up. Was she attempting to communicate? She made unfamiliar sounds he didn't understand.

Behind him in the dense foliage, branches rustled and birds cried out. No doubt Echo reminding him to return to the safety of the jungle. Tarzan ignored his brother and watched the female's eyes widen as she searched beyond his shoulder. He may not understand her, but perhaps she might understand him.

"*Ooh-uh*," he grunted, signing for her to follow him into the jungle and leave the unprotected openness of the beach.

Tarzan turned and knuckle-loped a few paces toward the trees covered with climbing ivy, then stopped and looked back.

She floundered in the deep sand, falling repeatedly to her knees. Finally, she glanced up, her eyes meeting his across the distance. Fatigue dimmed the light of her bright irises as she curled her legs under and sat her hip in the sand. In the full sun, the color of her drying hair lightened, nearly matching that of the windswept sand. The breeze blew strands across her face, and she pushed them back with tender, feminine grace.

The females in his family acted the same as this human, both particular about their grooming.

Branches at his back shook with a violent reminder to get back to the protection of the jungle canopy. Over his shoulder, Tarzan threw Echo a glare, then returned his attention to the little female. She'd never make it off the sand before the tide rose higher on the beach, possibly washing her away.

Before he could think twice, or his brother fell out of the tree, Tarzan used his knuckles to lope back and crouch beside her. Digging into the sand to gather her into his arms, he lifted her slight, squawking form and hurried into the cool green forest.

The female squirmed with his alpha male tactics, but once the comfort of thick foliage enfolded them in a blanket of safety, she settled and accepted aid.

A lineup of brightly colored beak-birds abandoned their perch when he rushed past. The female in his arms leaned her head back to follow the birds' upward flight. The smooth column of her throat lay fully exposed, and he wondered if she realized the submissive act she'd just performed. The hollow at the base of her neck drew his attention, he found the moisture on her skin from the heavy mid-morning air fascinating.

The trail he followed was nothing more than a thin line used by thousands of small four-legged animals, but it was as familiar to him as the weave of overhead vines. Before he tripped and dropped her, he'd best watch where he stepped.

Twigs snapped close behind, but he didn't turn to look. The four-beat thump with deep breathing would be Echo, his best friend and brother. When the trail dove under brush too small for a body his size, Tarzan gazed about for a nearby tree to climb.

"Where are you taking me?"

The soft murmur startled him. To talk when one should be quiet proved the female's necessity for his protection. He cut his gaze down at her and grunted for silence, once again moved by the color of her eyes.

Echo passed on Tarzan's left, ambling toward a stout tree layered with ancient bark. The ape's large hands gripped the coarse wood while his feet propelled his huge body upward.

"Oh, my God."

"*Uh*," Tarzan reprimanded.

At the first branch able to hold Echo's weight, his brother stopped and waited.

"You're not going up there, are you?"

In the undergrowth on the opposite side, leaves crunched as soft-padded feet stalked closer. No doubt attracted by the sound of her voice. Until she learned to remain silent, the canopy would be her only safe haven.

Tarzan released her legs and swung her lower body around to rest against his back. When she didn't instantly clamp her thighs around his waist, he grabbed her ankle and wrapped her leg into place. He paused until the softness of her body pressed into his back and her small heels dug into the muscles of his stomach.

Thoughts of her firm breasts filling his palm earlier hardened his mating tool. He'd watched other members of his family openly and frequently mate, then taken himself in hand to relieve his tool's pressure. Though he'd yet to experience the act with a female, he all too well understood the ritual of mating.

A deep, low growl rumbled from behind him. If he were alone, he'd turn to fight the cat who crept along in hopes of an ambush. But today, with his weak female barely clinging to his back, he'd take to the high branches of safety instead.

Facing the tree, Tarzan bent his legs as he'd been taught.

"Holy shit."

With a burst of energy, he leaped onto the tree at the same moment the female screamed and her arms tightened their cross-body hold.

J ane held on for all she was worth. The guy must be an extreme survivalist or something. After all, he'd jumped from the ground onto a fucking tree with her riding him piggyback!

Her mind spun with the possibility he might be a headhunter, but his features appeared European under all that black facial hair.

Before, when he'd lifted her out of the sand, she'd caught a fleeting glimpse of an irregular-shaped animal hide tied loosely around his hips. She wondered how long he'd lived alone since he seemed incapable of communication.

Then again, though they may not speak the same language, she knew the look that told her to shut up when she saw it.

His thick fingers gripped the roughened bark, and his feet found crevices for leverage. As if he were military trained in Special Forces, he quickly climbed the tree, her weight making little difference to the wild jungleman.

Below, a spotted jaguar paced a figure eight at the base of the tree, its yellow eyes glaring up at them as the cat yowled in frustration. *Cats climb trees, so why isn't this one?*

Jane readjusted her hold, tightening both knees to lift herself higher on his smooth, muscular back before she slid off completely. The rapid manner in which the man climbed took them a few dozen feet off the ground. Dizzy from the increasing height, she switched her gaze to glance up.

The reason for the jaguar's hesitation became immediately clear. High above, a huge silverback gorilla gripped a smaller branch for support as he stood on bowed legs and edged further out on a thick limb. The backward slope of his fur-covered head accentuated the protrusion of the ape's mouth, the same orifice where two long, white fangs threatened the closer they climbed.

They, meaning him.

"Oh crap. It just keeps getting better."

"*Uh.*"

Jane didn't need to see his eyes to know she'd been told to shut her yap—again.

Which proved hard to do when the man exited his tree-climbing *modus operandi* and moved onto the same solid-looking branch as the gorilla.

The great hairy beast continued to back away, weight behind each step gently bouncing the limb. Round black eyes watched warily as the animal's stare darted between the wild man and her.

Suddenly, the man grasped one of her ankles and made to unwind her leg from his torso. "*Ooh-ooh.*"

"Oh, hell no!" Jane scrambled to grip her thighs tighter than before. She didn't know which might be worse: A dangerous gorilla or a thousand species of spiders that inhabited a jungle.

"*Ooh-ooh.*" He grunted harder, shaking his back and tipping sideways at the waist.

A Rhesus monkey had nothing on her. No matter which way he leaned, no matter how hard he might shake, she'd be damned if she'd come off his back. Jungle-boy wanted her there in the first place, now he'd live with the consequences.

Besides, sure as shit if she put her bare feet down on the slippery limb, she would pitch head-over-ass off the side.

For good measure, Jane added a chokehold to make her message clear.

The branch dipped and swayed at the far end. "*Ooh-ooh-ooh.*"

The gorilla's large, black eyes stared at them as its lips pulled back in a snarl, showing all ninety-nine of its razor-sharp canines. In what Jane thought was an aggressive show of dominance, fists the size of sledgehammers alternated between pounding the limb between its wide-spaced feet and thumping his chest.

"You really pissed him off now," she hissed from her piggyback position.

Jungle-boy pulled her arm and, for one hair-raising moment, took his hand off the tree in order to pry her off his body.

Though he didn't dispel her, he'd managed to switch her position so her boobs pressed to his rock hard chest.

Nose to nose, Jane stared into his golden-flecked, surprised eyes. Noted the way his brows lowered and how he narrowed his eyes. She realized the moment his irritation drained out and heat moved in.

"*Ooh-uh-uh.*" He uttered the sounds in short, clipped tones.

The branch dipped dangerously, then suddenly sprang up, nearly pitching her off the side. Above Jane and to her right, the huge silverback rustled leaves and snapped twigs as he moved through a system of interwoven branches as languidly as if he walked down a sidewalk on Main Street. When he reached a long hanging vine, he grasped it one-handed, then turned to grunt a parting farewell. A simple step off into nothingness, and the great ape swung away.

Jane turned back to the jungle man again. "Did you see that? He just swung on a freaking vine."

Where did the gorilla go? She hoped he didn't go for reinforcements from his jungle-thug friends. Squirming to gain a better view, it slowly dawned on her that the man had gone completely still.

Chapter Three

His brother certainly lived up to his name. After vine-swinging away, his laughter echoed loudly in Tarzan's brain. The frightened female had mashed herself to his body, and no matter how hard he tried, he hadn't dislodged her. Like an infant gorilla, she'd ended up clinging to the front of his body.

A fact that hadn't gone unnoticed by his mating tool.

Her arms wrapped behind his neck while her ankles locked above his butt. Her light colored hair separated into sections and blew a strand across her mouth. He wondered if her hair, so different from his own, would feel as soft as it looked. A lock fluttered in the breeze, then wedged in the seam of her lips. He imagined the same sunshine-filled locks dragging up his thighs to caress between his legs.

Caught like a willing rabbit in her snare, Tarzan froze as desire flared in a burst of hot pulsing need. Beneath the protection of his animal skin cover, his male part rose as it grew in size and width. Soon, his tool would make its demands known.

"You have amazing eyes." The female's thighs loosened their grip, and her breasts slid down his chest.

Closer...closer.

"And your muscles...you're so strong."

Whatever she'd said, he wanted to hear more. The sound of her soft voice stirred a thrumming sensation inside him.

Tarzan reached behind himself to feel for the tree's trunk, then carefully leaned his back against the scratchy surface.

The female's arms unfolded and her body slid lower. "I hope there's no spiders up here."

Concerned she'd slip off entirely or lose her balance, he cupped his palms under the roundness of her butt. He'd intended to only protect her from falling out of the tree, but what his hands discovered would be forever imprinted in his memory.

The strange covering over her legs hid nothing from his touch. The female's butt fit in his hands perfectly as his fingers tightened on each side. He lifted her up, then slid her down, closer to his straining male need.

Her heels dug into the small of his back and she exhaled a breathy sigh.

Tarzan repeated the motion, which further hardened his mating tool.

The female closed her eyes and leaned her head back. "Oh my God..."

In the tree nests of his family group, he'd seen males touch the female's parts and test their readiness to mate.

Watching her closed eyes for any sign of refusal, Tarzan slid his hands lower, his fingers searching over the blue covering for the opening to her sex. He rubbed over the area several times, but found no opening. Frustrated, he pressed against the strange cloth that covered her secrets, wondering if he should tear the wrapper open.

"Damn. You don't know how to speak, but I don't think it matters. Let me down." She released the hold on his neck and wiggled her butt and legs.

Tarzan slid her core over his hardened tool, then waited.

Her eyes widened. A slow smile spread across her pretty face. "Like that, do you?"

His turn to close his eyes when she wiggled and rubbed again.

"You've been without a woman for too long."

"*Ooh-ooh.*"

At her wiggling insistence, he opened his eyes and reluctantly placed her on her feet.

Rather than risk falling, the female immediately knelt down on the wide branch. One hand wrapped around his ankle, she carefully glanced over the edge at the forest far below. "Jaguar's gone." She swung her attention back to him and stared at his lengthened male part. "And I have a feeling my clothes will be, too."

Whatever she'd said to his tool, it must have involved her mouth, because she licked her lips.

"*Uh-uh.*" He pulled on the flowered blue that covered her breasts, then pointed at the tougher shield over her legs. All females bore an opening through which the mating part slid in and out.

At the thought, his tool jumped. Tarzan wrapped his hand around the hardened length to subdue it.

"Here? In the tree?" With her brow wrinkled, the female appeared to become agitated again. "Seriously?"

He gazed down at her, wondering what caused such a reaction when moments before she was all sweet sounds and closed eyes—a sign of her readiness to mate. *Hmm.* It first happened when he'd touched the covering between her legs. Females in his family didn't like their hair stroked in the opposite direction. Perhaps it was the same for this human female.

For the sake of his heavy mating tool, he tried again, reaching to stroke a soothing path over her covered breast.

Her eye-skin drooped.

He did the same to her other breast.

More drooping.

"*Ooh-ooh.*" A smile pulled the edges of his mouth. He was getting the hang of this mating thing. But the breast cover wasn't his female's skin, and he wanted to know the softness for himself. He skimmed a finger over her dewy cheek, then tugged at her shoulder where the cover lay bunched up. How could he unwrap this succulent fruit? Unsure how to proceed, Tarzan straightened and leaned against the tree again, crossing his arms to think out the matter.

"Alright, I get it. You won't get me out of the tree until I take my clothes off. By the way, when's the last time you had a haircut?" After the female stopped her chatter and flashed a quick, lopsided smile, her hands grasped the bottom of the breast covering and slowly peeled the damp cloth over her head.

He reached to touch the blue-flowered material, surprised when she handed it to him. Bringing the limp cover to his nose, he closed his eyes and inhaled the female's scent deep inside to fill his senses. Sweet, like the treetop jungle after a warm rainstorm. He opened his eyes to see his female sweep the long fall of her doe-colored hair over one shoulder and reach behind her back.

Worried the tiny bugs that gave painful bites dared to latch onto her tender, pale skin, he ignored the coral-colored breast cover that she'd removed and stepped closer.

What caused his female to claw the skin between the bones of her shoulders? Standing before her, he grasped the back of her neck and pushed her low to see.

"What the hell?" his female squawked. "If you want something, just say it."

Other than a white line across her back where the skin appeared lighter than the rest, no biter bugs attacked. Just to be certain, he ran a flat palm across the creamy expanse to feel for bumps. Soft and warm, like a treetop daybed lined with moss. Except moss never caused his throbber to twitch in beat to his heart's pulse.

Confused at the source of her discomfort, Tarzan burrowed his fingers into her hair. He gently pulled her into a kneeling position, straightening her spine. Her cheek slid along the side of his hardened length.

As if an electric eel zapped the tip of his male part, he jerked his hips back and forth to ease the tingling sensation.

She stared at him, nose to throbbing tip. "Oh...boy."

Chapter Four

An impressive erection rose from beneath the sideways flap of a simple breechcloth. Jane didn't need spoken words to understand what his pumping hips said.

Jungle-boy wanted sex.

Preferably oral sex.

The fist in her hair loosened and she glanced up, wondering if she'd read his body language correct. His eyes were two volcanoes of smoldering lava, staring down at her from his towering height.

Had any man ever looked at her with such devastating need? No, never. She'd never been particularly pretty, her figure tilted toward the well-fed side. Too many hours sitting at her desk and not enough time enjoying the great outdoors.

Currently, a non-issue.

Jungle-boy's beard grew bushy and wild. Bits of dried leaves littered the length that hung like bristling ivy down to his neck. Above his hair-covered lips and a nose that'd been broken, his heated eyes drew Jane.

The boisterous squall of birds split the air a moment before a colorful flock of parrots surged past the tree limb from their roost below. A feline's shriek added to the cacophony of noise.

Moving her hands over the rough tree bark to adjust her position, pain burst from the raw injury in her left palm as though her flesh were on fire. She opened her mouth, crying out. The fist tightened in the hair at the side of her head and jammed her face against his bulging package.

If he'd wanted a bullseye, then he'd missed his shot.

Pushing back against his hand, she turned her face in order to breathe. Long, hard, and velvety soft, the man's penis jutted out in direct contact to her lips. Sounds of the jungle fell away, as did the sting of her hand and the rough bark scratching her legs.

"*Ooh-ooh,*" he grunted faintly, twisting his hips left and right as he turned to survey the jungle.

"Medieval—"

The hand in her hair tightened and pushed her mouth harder against his shaft. With her nose smashed against the smooth skin of his rippled lower abs, she opened her mouth to breathe around the veiny-thick width of him and took her first taste of untamed jungle.

He swiveled his hips.

Jane's tongue slid toward the puffy end and back again.

"*Uh...*" His hips pressed forward, the swivel of his pelvis moved slower, more pronounced.

Jane closed her mouth over his heated length, relishing the feel of silk over steel. A second hand joined his first to cup the back of her head. His seductive thrusts heated her from the inside out.

Careful of her injured palm, she lifted one hand to massage his sensitive balls while the other gripped his ass. At the next slide toward his swollen head, she darted her tongue out to lick at the underside of the tip.

Saliva gathered in the back of her throat, preparing her mouth to take him fully inside. Desire to slide his thickness between her lips caused a moan to slip out, and her eyes drifted shut. The heady combination of his muscle-corded butt and a baby-soft sac wreaked havoc with opposite tactile sensations.

She wanted so much more. Opening her mouth, she sucked at the side of his damp erection.

He pulled her hair at the same time as he withdrew his stiffness inches from her mouth. Jane tried to reach for it with her tongue and let out a breath of frustration when she couldn't. Glancing up in question, she watched his gaze dart to the ground below.

Vigilant. Alert.

His expression appeared serious as he studied the jungle around them, and then that same intent gaze turned to her.

Heat-filled latte eyes stared deeply into hers. Below the untamed crop of facial hair, his lips pressed a thin line. He didn't blink, he didn't move. For a few wild heartbeats, the man stood as still as a statue; cock jutted proudly, fingers gripping her hair.

Upon the next swivel, his hips angled to the right, and Jungle-boy's drool-worthy asset faced Jane straight on.

Hey! Hello! How are you today?

That's what his nodding erection seemed to say. By no means had Jane ever been one of *those* women, the type who slept with different men like the days of the week. Didn't mean she lacked a healthy sexual appetite, conveniently fed by the latest in adult toy inventions.

The big-girl plaything that hung deliciously close, precum weeping from the tip, proclaimed a satisfaction guarantee to her heated core.

Normal sounds of the living jungle registered in Tarzan's mind. Hollow resonances of gorillas beating their chests merged with the drone of a million insects. Every day chatter, blending one into the other.

The trees and vines and all the living creatures were his home. Vital to his existence and that of his ape family.

None of it mattered as much as what his female would do next with her mouth.

Laps from her soft tongue along the sides of his hardened shaft was agony in perpetual bliss. The sun sifted through the canopy's swaying leaves to splash her in varying shades of shadow and light. She licked her lips, the pink tongue darting out to tease his resistance, breaking him down one heartbeat at a time.

Her hungry eyes climbed up his body and met his. "Can I? What would you do if I did?"

The unique color in the intensity of her stare drew his attention. If only they could communicate, he'd tell her that lying down to mate in a sun nest would be more comfortable than balancing on a bare limb. He traced the backs of his knuckles along a whitish line the ocean left upon her cheek. *Fragile.*

She opened her mouth and dragged in a stuttered breath, then slid her steamy gaze down.

Heat scorched his male sex from within, tightening his butt and thrusting his need.

Her hair slithered forward and hid her features from his view.

Tarzan pushed the long strand back, leaving his fingers buried in the softness at the crown of her head. The muscles under his balls clenched, begging him to either take himself in hand or turn the female around. Another drop of male juice seeped out to join the first.

"Just don't kill me."

Mesmerized by her slow, deliberate movement, he watched in fascination as his female tilted back her head, opened her mouth like a blossoming flower, and stuck out her tongue. The drip from the tip lengthened, stretching as the juices pulled to meet her seeking lips.

The longer the fluid hovered over the female's open mouth, the tighter his balls squeezed. The ache of his extended male part increased painfully. He pulled his hand from her hair to grip his throbbing shaft at the base.

A third droplet formed at the slit, pushing forward that which came before it. When the single drip finally touched her outstretched tongue, she slowly raised up on her knees to gather the remaining fluid and lick the droplets up.

Hot pleasure speared from the end of his sex, shot past his tightly gripped fist, and filled his balls with a mating desire that couldn't be restrained. She licked him again, using the tip of her tongue to fondle the underside of the plumed head. He pulled his hips back, letting the hardened length slide through his fist, then shot forward just as fast.

"*Ooh-ooh-ooh.*" Tarzan tightened the hand he'd left tangled in her hair. Pushing ever so gently, he showed her in the language they'd adopted how he wanted her to lick him again.

His next breath caught in the tightness of his chest as she flicked her gaze up to his, and then back down to his swollen maleness.

She licked him. Softly at first and just on the end. Then she pursed her lips in the manner his family used to test the texture of suitable fruit.

I'm ripe. I'm very ripe.

In the same slow, agonizing pace she'd been using, she pressed her lips to the head of his throbbing groin snake and slid him into her mouth. Smooth as honey and hot as the steam pools, he watched as more and more of his male part disappeared past the seam of her rosy lips.

Beak-birds screeched, songbirds sang. A pattering tapped the large shady leaves all around. Tarzan glanced up, he hadn't noticed the dimming of light and clouds moving in overhead. Light rain sprinkled down, hushing the heat insects to bring forth others who relished the cleansing water.

Warm hands touched his thighs and slid over his skin toward her sucking mouth. He peered down until the backward drag of her tongue forced him to close his eyes. Like the tree at his back, he stood immobile, afraid that if he moved, she'd startle and stop.

Forward and back, she sucked his length in, her tongue rubbing along his shaft from within. He cupped the female's head and increased his grip as a familiar pressure grew below. His thighs spread wider on their own and his knees bent slightly.

"Mmm." Her tongue rolled a circle around him, sucking the end she held in her mouth. Down she went and then back up, not as slow as before. Her injured hand gently held his balls while the other pushed his fingers out of the way to grip the hard mating length on her own. Her hand slid and twisted as she went up and down. Her mouth skimmed faster with each stroke.

"*Ooh-ooh-ooh!*" Unable to control the muscles in his butt, he pushed forward with his hips and pulled down with his hands.

The female didn't fight his control for mating, she seemed ready to accept his insertion. After a few more pumps, he pulled her mouth away and quickly moved to stand behind her.

Tarzan set his palm between the warm skin of her shoulder blades and pushed until her hands settled on the wide surface of the tree limb. To test her mating readiness, he lowered to one knee behind her round butt and followed the examples of his gorilla family by rubbing between the female's legs.

She immediately pushed toward him, arching her back and thrusting her hips skyward. "Pants...off." Suddenly, the female twisted, scratching at her waist.

Tarzan straightened from his bent position as the cover wrapping her hips loosened and slipped down her thighs.

Chapter Five

Maybe it's because she'd cheated death after being left behind on a sinking yacht. Or perhaps it was the untamed jungle, filled with animals, and a lone wildman loosened her inhibitions.

Then again... Jane twisted to look over her shoulder at the virile beast of a man who brought every shipwrecked fantasy to life.

She pushed an extra vertebra into the arch of her back, adding the extra *oomph* to her ongoing primal request.

The sight widened Jungleman's eyes and his nostrils flared. With slow, hesitant movements, he leaned down for a closer look. "*Ooh.*"

Turned on and close to exploding, she faced forward, unable to watch the curious flight of emotions ripple across his face. Water dripped from her bangs and she closed her eyes, shaking her rain-wet hair. His touch, though light as a breeze, swamped her core as his single finger traced a straight line down from her anus.

He pressed against the frame of her swollen sex as if he were testing the ripeness of fruit. "*Ooh-ooh.*"

She heard a sniffing sound. "Oh, god," she groaned aloud, imagining him scenting her *there*. If he could smell how turned on she was in the middle of a rainforest jungle, then his face must be—her moan turned into words, "Oh, yeah."

Carefully, slowly, his hand touched her heated essence. The very part of her that clenched in an animalistic need. Continuing the brain-numbing exploration, he pushed harder and his fingers slipped inside.

If Jungleboy didn't hurry his wild-ass up, she'd go bat-shit crazy and scream like the monkeys that hung from the trees. "Get on with it," Jane hissed through her gritted teeth. To encourage a faster pace, she pushed back and deepened the plunge of his fingers.

The wildman's reaction was immediate. A pumping of air in and out of his lungs with a half dozen *ooh-ooh's* thrown in.

He wiggled his buried fingers, which tapped her G-spot, and it was Jane's turn to moan a call of the wild.

Raucous calls of trumpeting birds drowned out the sound of her voice. Monkeys echoed in return to increase the crescendo of noise.

He pulled his fingers from her body and for a moment, Jane thought he might leave her. A quick glance over her shoulder told a different story.

Eyes blazing with molten heat, he fisted his cock in his big hand. The back-and-forth stare between his extended sex and where she wanted him most made it seem like he wasn't quite sure what to do.

Taking matters into her own hands, she lowered her upper body to rest on the tree and widened the spread of her legs.

Then waited.

"*Ooh.*" The limb bounced, his legs dragged closer. "*Uh-uh.*"

Tropical heat, in the form of a jungle man, nudged her slick opening.

"*Ooh.*"

"Put it in already!" Jane reached between her legs and opened herself wider with two fingers to maximize his viewing pleasure.

His lungs pumped an excited heavy breathing, punctuated with his ape-like *ooh-ooh-ooh's*.

"Enough with the—" *Yesss!* Hard as stiffened silk, his thick length filled her aching body. Pressure collided with the clench of her tiny inner muscles. Strong hands gripped the sides of her hips and held tight.

Seated deep within, he stilled.

And then all bets were off.

In a rapid motion, Jungleboy pushed and pulled, grunting the only word he seemed to say.

Jane had to lift her face away from the tree or risk an evergreen form of jungle dermabrasion.

After all the waiting, after the slow-motion movements and his careful study of how Protrusion A goes into Slot B, the wait would soon be over.

Just a few more hard-driving thrusts...to send her over...the....

"*Ahh-yahyahyah-yah-ahh!*" The wildman's howl broke the steamy jungle air like a sonic boom.

He thrust hard. He thrust deep.

He keeled over and lay panting across her perspiring back.

"Wait, no!" Jane cried, backward bumping him with her hips. She pushed against his deflating organ in a futile attempt to gain Nirvana. "No, no, no! You're not done yet."

"*Ooooh...*" Jungle-disappointment slid off and lay on his back, draped in a precarious position over the branch with his shoulders and legs hanging off either side.

Stunned, her core pulsing like a greedy kid who'd had a favorite toy taken away, she turned to stare at him in disbelief...and just a little bit pissed-off.

Chapter Six

No wonder my ape family lay in treetop nests all day—breeding took the energy of an elephant.

Tarzan opened his eyes. Through the crisscross weave of tree limbs above, the weather cleared, and blue sky peeked between white, puffy clouds.

Good day...for a nap. He adjusted his arms for better balance, sleep dragging his eye-skin closed.

"Ahem."

"*Uh.*" He grunted his annoyance. The female was worse than Echo, who could be heard three vine swings away, beating his puny excuse of a chest.

Day sleep, his mother used to say, put a banana back into the peel.

Tarzan didn't understand it any better now than he had back then, but somehow she made more sense than before. He crossed his ankles, enjoying the light breeze that wafted up from the jungle floor and caressed the bottoms of his feet.

"Wake up."

"*Grr.*" The growl rumbled in his throat longer than necessary. Tarzan hoped she'd take the hint.

"Don't give me that snarling crap," she hissed in a whispered tone. "Get up!"

Whatever had gotten the female excited, her nonstop chattering seemed to worsen with time. He cracked open an eye to see her pressed back against the main stalk of the tree, her leg covering down around her ankles. The color in her pretty face paled as she peered frantically at the jungle floor below.

Hair rose on the back of his neck, and not because he lay hanging from the limb. A darker tone sped up the beat of his heart, and he opened his other eye.

The female's now bare leg stretched toward his ribs, her toes pointed, trying to kick the part of him that lay out of her reach. Her foot wiggled his direction, and it was as if the clouds parted and the heat of the sun shone down. Between her legs flashed the most beautiful sight he'd never tire of seeing—moist, pink, and everything he'd ever wanted. If he weren't so tired….

The air hung shrouded, heavy and still. Birds remained silent and hidden from view. Long-tailed monkeys were strangely quiet.

Weariness vanished as instinct rose. He rolled toward his female, onto his stomach. The top of her foot connected in a sharp slap to the back of his shoulder. He turned to glare at her, then swiveled to look down when several twigs snapped.

A set of footsteps crunched leaves moments before a male human with skin darker than Tarzan's emerged from behind the wide-leafed plants. Over his upper body, a covering matched the color of the sea but did little to blend with the surrounding jungle. He moved carefully, searching after every few steps.

The female slid closer, her foot scraping the length of his leg. "Do you see him?"

"*Ooh,*" he cut in reply. Would she ever have the good sense to stay silent?

An anxious crease deepened between her brows as she quietly chattered, eyes searching the leafy ground like the little nut gatherers.

Much the same as the steamy jungle came alive when a new day brightened, the melody of her voice strung lilting tones together. Tarzan longed to understand her sounds of communication. For the sake of the female's survival, he needed to find a way.

"He's one of the pirates."

"...*Ritz.*" His tongue rolled over the unfamiliar tones.

The blue of her eyes lost some of their fear when she turned suddenly to stare at him. Clean, slim fingers tucked a long group of hair behind her delicate ear, and a corner of her mouth lifted. "You spoke."

"*Sss..poke.*"

Guttural human clamor from the jungle floor caused Tarzan to clench his teeth and tighten his muscles. Unlike the songbird pitch of his female, the enemy's mouth-sounds set him on edge.

Danger sprang from every pore of the advancing male; from the manner in which he stalked, to the way his guarded eyes searched the leaves of every jungle plant.

Undergrowth snapped as an object moved undisguised through the thickness. A second dark-skinned male joined the first, an off-white covering hung in tatters over a reed-thin body. By rapid hand movements and loud voices, they communicated through their harsh mouth-sounds, pointing long sticks in different directions.

A short distance away came the thumps of gorilla chest drumming. Another replied, this one closer and offbeat. *Echo, no doubt.*

The inane silence of the usually raucous rainforest pricked at Tarzan's stretched nerves.

From yet another direction, a third human male appeared. Shoulders draped in a loose-fitting red mantel, he moved with a confident stride, even and smooth. Rather than crash through the dense, damp growth, he picked his way carefully as he targeted a specific path. When he reached his friends, the male adjusted the thick belt at his waist.

The female drew closer on her knees, her flowery scent drifting in the air. Too much movement and she would draw the males' attentions.

Tarzan reached his hand and gripped her small wrist, his thumb circling past the knuckles of his fingers. He conveyed through his lowered brows that she should remain motionless. The blue of her wide eyes once again startled him, after years of having only seen brown staring back.

She opened her mouth, and reflexively, he clamped his lips tight, pushing his mental image to remain silent. Her moist face, pale and smooth, set off the pink of her petal-soft lips.

The lips that took his mating tool deep inside her mouth.

Water dripped from the trees towering above, thick air clogged his breath. Sounds of movement from below pried his gaze away from eyes he could stare into throughout the light time. As long as he and his female remained completely still, they'd be safe.

The trio strode single-file in the direction where the first male had appeared, toward the sea.

Beside him, his female released a gusty breath. "That was close." She pulled on her wrist he held clamped in his hand. Until bird song filled the air, he and the female would remain where they were. "Now what?"

"*Uh-uh.*" Tarzan pointed down at the tree limb and settled himself into a more comfortable position to wait.

She tugged her arm again, and when he didn't release her, he watched fascinated as her facial features began to change.

The top line of her mouth turned down and her chin jutted forward. She narrowed her eyes to stem-thin slits. *So, she is angry again. An attitude he was becoming familiar with.*

The instant mood shift when she didn't get her way wasn't so much irritating as it was captivating. *She could glare pointed stickers into his skin, and he would still find her pleasing to the eye.* He rubbed his free hand over the hair at his mouth, absorbing the thoughts of his wandering mind.

When he was a youthling and storm clouds filled his ape mother's eyes, he would set out to gather her favorite leaves or a sweet fruit to eat. The gifts always pushed her anger away.

Would this also work for a human female?

He had to try before the less-than-friendly glares shrank his mating tool further.

One after another, the twitter of songbirds reemerged to engage the silent jungle. Tarzan released her and gathered his legs under himself, then rose to a squatting position. He patted the scratchy log, watching as she rubbed her skin where he'd gripped her wrist.

Patting the limb again, he pointed to emphasize. "*Ooh.*"

"Yes, tree. I get it."

"*Ay-geddit.*" His thick tongue stumbled over the new sounds.

Water from her hair dripped down the side of her nose. She stuck out her tongue to catch the drop, then licked her lips for more.

"*Ah-ah.*" He could have banged his hollow head against the massive tree. His female thirsted! Of course she did. She'd come from the water that puckered his lips.

Tarzan pulled her to her feet as he straightened to his full height. Reaching for the vine that grew long, curled leaves, he grabbed the nearest frond and then tapped her lips. When she pulled away, he opened his mouth to show her and poured a small amount of water onto his tongue.

Like an infant bird, she opened wide, and he tilted the leaf to drizzle rainwater in. He pulled another leaf, and when she drank it all, he pulled yet another. Several mouthfuls later, she closed her eyes and let out a satisfied sigh.

And then her stomach growled.

Her eyes flew open, she lifted her gaze and smiled shyly. "Yeah, I'm hungry, too."

Relieved the female's irritation passed without the use of gifts, Tarzan smiled in return. The few wormy insects caught in the rainwater would do nothing to stop the complaint of her empty gut. As an accomplished hunter, he would fill her stomach and show her what an extraordinary provider she'd chosen as her mate.

Chapter Seven

Jungleboy ignored her when Jane asked where he was going. He had grabbed a thick vine, flashed a cocky smile, then pushed off from the branch she'd been left to perch on.

"Ugh, whatever." At least the cool water had refreshed her raw throat. She hadn't even minded the bits of dirt.

What bothered her was knowing that the pirates, or whoever they were, had survived the sinking of the boat and were now looking for her. With rifles. All she had for protection was a non-English speaking wildman who swung on vines and left her body craving for more.

At least she was safe up high in a tree.

What a minute. She smacked her lips and leaned over the curve of the limb to glance down three stories. *There's no dirt up here.*

Before an overactive imagination drop-kicked her stomach into riding the Heaving Highway, Jane inhaled deeply through her nose. The jungle, with all its wonderful, natural smells, reminded her she was still alive.

Even if she sat stuck in a tree with no apparent way down.

To add to her five-hanky-tale-of-woe, she had no way of knowing whether or not the guy would be coming back for her. He'd simply patted the tree and grunted, as if he'd told her to stay put.

Perhaps it'd been wishful thinking on her part.

It might also be the way his people said, "*Sayonara* sucker."

Remembering how both the giant silverback ape and her jungle man moved through the trees, Jane glanced around for a similar rope-like vine. She spied one further out on the limb at what she hoped was less than an arm's length away.

To keep her balance and not topple to her death, she dropped to her hands and knees.

The crawling shuffle separated her pants from her ankle and dispatched her denim capris to bomb the plants below.

"No, no, no..."

The red lace panties followed, fluttering down at a slower, more sedate pace. She would have to retrieve them and her blouse once her feet touched *terra firma*. At least she still had a bra to wear. One *small* article of clothing kept her from feeling totally vulnerable and naked.

Moving like an ant, but feeling like an elephant in a tree, the broad limb bounced with her forward movements. False confidence intact, she inched her way along. Four strides into it, the limb narrowed substantially. Just a few more feet and she could reach the vine.

A bait-ball of frenzied gnats floated up as a buzzing grey fog and tumbled over each other as they raced toward her in a crash collision. Attracted by her salty sweat, her face made like a windshield with struggling little bugs stuck to her skin.

"Shit!" She sat up and swiped at her cheeks. "I fucking hate the jungle."

Not finished yet, a few of the insects flew into her mouth. Jane spat several times and shook her head, hoping her long hair would act like a horse's tail and swish them away. She batted the air in front of her face with both hands, daring a glance toward the hanging vine.

Creeping forward on her knees, performing the hand-jive as a screen for her face, she kept her eye on the prize.

To her right was a thirty-foot drop to a jungle floor littered with sharp rocks, gun-wielding pirates, and more insects. On her left, hanging like a long green boa constrictor, a thick vine stretched toward the ground. If she ever wanted something to eat, she needed to leave the treetop canopy.

Sorry, Jungleboy. For all its wonderful views and safety, trees were for the birds and gorillas, of which she was neither.

Jane rubbed her eyes to remove the last of the little bug bodies, then carefully stuck her arm out, over the abyss, and reached sideways for the vine. Like everything else in the humid jungle, a moist barrier lay between her palm and the plant.

As if they cheered her on, brightly colored parrots squawked as they flew onto nearby branches to perch and watch. A hollow drumming beat in the distance, followed by deep growls reminiscent of the jungle man.

Something of a blend between zip lining and a bungee jump, the trick would be glomming onto the vine with both hands while swinging from her perch. Wild Thing made it look so easy, just grab and go.

"I got this." *No problemo.*

The vine was heavier than she'd first thought as she strained to pull the stalk toward the limb. Below her, the tail of the plant swung as if it were a living entity. *Well, it is a living thing*, she corrected herself.

Jane just hoped she would still be a living *thing* by the time she hit the jungle floor.

After a few test tugs to flay the truckload of apprehension coursing through her veins, she shimmied around so her bare butt sat the on the branch with her legs hanging over. "It'll be worth every splinter if this works." She grasped the bulky vine in both hands, her feet curled and caught the slippery length. All she had left to do was slide off the limb and glide to the ground.

No sweat.

"One for the money, two for the show." Jane took a deep breath. "Three to get ready, and four to *gooo*!"

Rough tree bark burned a road-rash onto the tender skin of her ass as she forced herself to slide off the limb. Her heart pounded a sped-up version of Taps in her throat. She tightened her hands and gripped the vine, the weightlessness of her thighs morphed her stomach into screaming *OHMYGOD!*

Sudden fear stunned her shell-shocked system, ripping a scream from the bottom of her curled toes.

The vine dropped with her weight, plummeting her shipwrecked life toward certain death. Still, she held on, afraid to let go. Waiting for the inevitable to kill her instantly.

From a downward drop to a pendulum arc, the vine caught and held as she sailed through the air.

Panic multiplied exponentially when a hairy black tarantula scrambled over her wrist. She opened her mouth for a terrified shriek that erupted straight from her soul.

Jane flung out her arm, which dislodged the spider, but her remaining hand lost its grip on the moist vine.

Tarzan piled the squirrels he'd speared onto the sweet fruit his mother preferred and pulled together the corners of the human female's upper body covering. Satisfaction spread like sun-warmed honey, knowing that he alone provided for his mate.

When she saw the results of his hunter-gatherer skills, he hoped she would *show* her appreciation.

He'd left her high in a tree with no lower branches. A safe location away from dangerous animals and predatory human males. Slipping the bundle's tied ends over the tip of his spear, he straightened and hefted their meal to one shoulder.

A short distance away, Echo sat hunched on a boulder, scratching his thigh as he waited for Tarzan to finish. His gorilla brother had followed the trespassing humans until they returned to a small boat and rowed away. As Echo drew closer, he regarded him through watchful eyes. His gaze flicked to the wrapped bundle. "*Ooh.*"

Tarzan couldn't remember a day when he'd felt so good. He tilted his head, inviting Echo to join him on the trek back to his female.

The silverback leaped down from the rock, narrowly missing him. His black lips pulled back and he brushed a hairy arm against Tarzan's shoulder. Side by side, they journeyed, quietly communicating in their way of body language and soft grunts. Following a small animal trail up the side of a steep slope, they stopped to rest at the crest.

A high-pitched scream split the air.

Tarzan jumped to his feet. His heart raced as he pumped his legs faster across knee-high grass to where the sound originated...The safe haven where he'd left his human mate.

If he hadn't been familiar with her cry from earlier, he might have mistaken what he'd heard for the spotted cat.

Behind him, Echo's fists and feet pounded the ground as he followed, intent on guarding his back.

Dashing toward her, he sprinted faster than he'd ever run before. Never in his life had he been so afraid. His brother's labored breaths faded away as blood pounded in his ears. Basic instinct propelled Tarzan to his mate.

Ahead, her pale body clung to a thin swinging vine that narrowly missed a tree. On the upward sweep, one of her hands lost its grip. She let go of another long, drawn-out shriek while her arm trailed uselessly in the air.

And then she was falling.

Tarzan leapt over the base of a leaning tree and used the trunk of another to kick himself into the air. His female's flailing arm struck the side of his head, but he caught her mid-air in his arms. The impact of her body hit him square in the chest, thrusting the air from his lungs.

Somehow, he was able to land on his feet.

He stumbled a few steps, then stopped to kneel before his legs buckled out from under him. Swamped with a whirl of emotions he didn't understand, he laid his cheek against his female's soft hair. Her slender shoulders trembled as she mewed tiny, damp gasps into the crook of his neck.

Echo ambled closer, keeping a respectful distance but curious all the same. He studied her hair and legs, touching his own to show the contrast in their differences.

"*Ooh.*" Tarzan tightened the hold on his female with one arm and rubbed circles over her back with the other.

Yes, he understood Echo's reference to her appearance, but he bore no resemblance whatsoever to his gorilla family as well. He would take this human female as his mate and protect her with his life. From the moment he set eyes on her, he'd felt a connection. A *something* greater than what he'd known within his family band.

"You saved me." Water in her eyes sparkled like raindrops before catching in her lashes to slip down her cheeks. "You made it look so easy. I thought I could do it too."

"*Doo-eetoo.*" Tarzan mimicked back.

The unfamiliar sounds brought a shaky smile to her face.

Echo knuckle-walked a few steps closer to sniff the air. Eager to learn more, he offered the back of his hand as he approached.

"*Uh-ooh,*" he said when she pressed closer to the protection of his body.

His brother stopped immediately but continued to offer his hand.

Slowly, his brave little female extended her arm and touched the back of her hand to Echo's.

Transfixed, his brother's intelligent eyes examined her hand. His gaze traveled up her arm until they sat staring at each other while their hands brushed.

Tarzan's arm started to ache, so he resettled his female to sit upright.

She smiled as she made herself comfortable in his lap. "My name is Jane." She tapped her fingers above the rosy tips of her breasts. "Jane."

"Jay-een."

"*Ooh.*"

At Echo's response, her clean white teeth appeared as her smile widened. "Jane."

"Jane." This time, the sound came more easily to Tarzan's tongue.

Echo's gaze bounced between the two of them. "*Ooh.*"

Jane touched her fingers to his chest, making his skin sizzle. "What's your name?"

"Jane."

He liked the way she tilted her head back, offering the slim column of her throat, and laughed. Echo joined with a howl of his own, which pulled up the corners of Tarzan's lips.

When her attention returned to him, she pressed her open palm to the swells of her breasts. "Jane."

Then she tapped the tips of her fingers against his chest and looked at him expectantly. She repeated the action and again, waited, leaving the heat of her touch to scorch his skin.

In the gorilla band, he didn't have a name. Only his position in the family. But a long time ago, one was given to him when he happened upon an ancient human male who'd stopped overnight on their island. The man had taken a stick and traced symbols in the sand, then called him by name.

It'd been many, many seasons since he'd last formed the word.

"Tar-zan."

Chapter Eight

Hypnotic and deep, his voice rumbled past his moistened lips and caressed Jane's cheeks. "Tarzan. What a lovely name."

Beneath the wiry facial hair, a corner of his mouth twitched. Strong angular features with widespread eyes.

She wondered what he might look like without the beard and given a decent haircut. She laid a finger at the top of his jaw and traced down, feeling the bone structure as she went.

"Jane." He repeated her motion, softly outlining her face with his hand.

What was it about this wild jungle man that brought out her primal need to mate? He smelled of earth and jungle, his dreadlock hair lay in a tangled mess. And lord only knew what hid within his beard.

Still...there was *something* between them. She lightly traced the bump in his nose and followed the slight curve as it bent to the left. His thick black lashes framed intelligent brown eyes that held flecks of gold in their depths.

His tongue darted out to wet his lips, and Jane's core tightened in response. Her nipples tingled seconds before the tips stiffened into hard little peaks.

Tarzan's gaze darted to the change in her body. His eyes darkened as he sniffed the air. Could he scent her arousal? His hand slid down the side of her throat to curl and support the weight of her breast. He plucked her nipple, tugging the sensitive tip.

An RSVP quaked between her thighs.

As if knowing how the primitive foreplay ignited her passion, he stared into her eyes and continued to skim past each bump of her ribs. His rough palm slid over the soft swell of her tummy, down to the place he'd ventured before. Lips parting to inhale as his lust bloomed, Tarzan glided his fingers between her wet folds and buried them deep inside.

"*Ooh-ooh.*" The same silverback gorilla she'd first seen earlier in the tree sat on his haunches and watched. His whiskey-colored eyes seemed to miss nothing as he took in the placement of Tarzan's hand. He lifted his huge, hairy arm to slap the ground, and then motioned his palm in the air. "*Ooh-ah-ooh-ah!*"

Suddenly, Tarzan became invigorated by the tone and actions of the great ape, grunting back *ooh-ooh-ooh* on panted breaths. Gently to not hurt her, but not without haste, he lifted and positioned her on the ground.

Sharp rocks bit into her back. Jane started to push herself up with her arms, but the jungle man quickly lay on top and wedged his hips between her legs. His lower body rocked as his hardened sex rooted for her core. Forever cautious, his eyes never stopped searching for possible signs of danger.

Not even as he took her.

This was domination at its basic, primal state, and Jane understood from her earlier study of primates. She accepted the uncomfortable rocks at her back and spread her bent legs in submission. Tarzan's frenzied movements to copulate were animalistic, yet indicative of how he'd been raised.

She calmly raised her hips and welcomed the brutal force of his entry. His thick cock plunged in and out, taking her in front of the loud ape who bounced thudding leaps off the ground in approval.

The act, vehement in appearance, demanded she respect who he was. If she remembered her college anthropology class correctly, Jungleboy's rutting act announced to the male population that she, Jane Porter, was Tarzan's property, and she was not to be touched.

Damn if she wasn't turned on by it all.

Combined grunts of excited primary beasts echoed in the thick jungle air. The screeches of monkeys lent their soprano voices to the deep bass of the gorillas. Above her, Tarzan's gaze burned into hers. He held himself balanced with two stiffened arms planted on either side of her shoulders. Under the thin veneer of tanned skin, his upper body muscles gleamed a humid sheen under the afternoon sky.

The force of his heated stare left her face to glance quickly about them again. Forever vigilant and always on guard, she would always be safe with him.

Jane raised her bent legs higher and brought her feet into the air. She gripped Tarzan's forearms and relished the feel of the trembling power she found. He gritted his teeth and closed his eyes. Sweat tracked along the sides of his face.

"Tarzan!" Her own body tightened, clenching the solid rod that hammered at her core.

His eyes flew open. He stopped fucking her long enough to adjust their position. Sitting back on his heels, he lifted her by the hips and held her lower body off the ground. An inhuman growl erupted from his throat. A move of supreme strength dragged her uplifted pelvis back and forth over his engorged sex.

In this new exchange, it was he who remained still and she who he manipulated to provide himself the greatest pleasure at the right speed and height.

Gravel dug into her flesh as her shoulders scraped the ground. Jane didn't care. Pleasure bloomed from the focal point where their bodies connected.

Never had she felt so female in a male-dominated world.

She spread her legs wider, giving him greater visual access to their public display. Tarzan's eyes dipped, his expression turned to stone as he watched himself plunge in and out of her wet channel. In her mind, she imagined the shine on his veiny surface.

His fingers bruised her skin as he slammed her harder onto his demanding sex—and she loved every pounding moment.

Two lines etched between his eyes as he lowered his brows. His expression took on that of an athlete determined to finish the race. Open-mouthed, he stared at the working action of his cock, chanting in time to his cadence, *"Ooh-ooh-ooh."*

The squeeze of her inner muscles tightened like a fist, clutching at a rod hard enough to drive nails. She had to peak. Through no fault of his own, he had denied her last time when he'd exploded too soon. Moaning loudly, Jane reached down between their bodies and touched her swollen nub.

A light back and forth brush against the bundle of nerves was all it took. Fulfillment detonated with her cry of pleasure as a spring of liquid joy burst forth.

Below his stiffened tool, his balls drew up snug. Tarzan closed his eyes and clenched his jaw, every muscle in his body tightening with the need for release. He might chip a tooth, but he'd hold it off, sparing more time to enjoy the feel of her—a hot hand squeezing around him.

"Tarzan!"

He inhaled deeply, the sweet scent of flowers mingling with the musk of his mate, Jane. Her sexual arousal bloomed in the air, permeated the breeze, and infused his senses. His fingers gripped the smooth surface of her skin, digging into the creased hollow where hip and thigh joined.

The moment his knees had hit the ground with Jane in his arms, his mating tool throbbed. A waterfall of relief for her safety produced an urgent need to feel his bare skin against hers.

When he'd sunk his fingers between her legs and into the hot depth of her body, the wetness he'd encountered sent spears of heat jolting through him. A physical slam sent straight to his throbbing organ and aching balls.

He pulled hard on her hips, ramming inside, stuffing her full of himself. Jane moaned again, the tight little sound echoed in his mind. Her hands lifted to slide a caress from his shoulders to his wrists, where she held on with a desperate, tight grip.

In and out, he worked her warm, wet body. The inner walls, slippery with her juices, pulsated as it gripped him.

Then, she lifted her knees and opened her legs wider. The sight of her wet, needy pink center watered his mouth for a taste. Next time he would lap the length of her moistened female sex.

Right now, however, his mating tool enjoyed spreading her flesh and the feel of her mating slit clamp around him.

A sensation of being burned alive with the sweetest of heat consumed him.

"*Uh-uh!*" On the outside of his periphery, Echo jumped up and down, urging him to hurry and finish.

The public mating was necessary to ensure that Jane remained his mate, and solely his. Only a protective brother would understand the necessity of hastening the action.

To solidify his stand, Tarzan chanted the alpha cry, sending the message to all primates. "*Ooh-ooh-ooh.*"

Other primates joined in, acknowledging the dominance he held over the female he mated. The jungle came alive as trees shook and voices carried.

Tarzan held onto Jane and pumped her body onto his.

Faster, harder.

She moaned loudly. Her legs drew back further, spread wider. She brought her hand forward to touch herself above where his mating tool impaled her sweet body.

Suddenly, her back arched off the ground. The muscles inside her slick, wet channel constricted to the point he struggled to drag in and out of her. His length gripped by unimaginable softness, he floated on the pleasure of sinking in and pulling out.

Jane closed her eyes tightly and cried out. Warm honey flowed, coating his mating tool and easing their friction of movement.

The essence of his mate hit Tarzan's nose with the effect of a charging bull elephant. He dipped his fingers in her female nectar to taste her body, to *know* her inside and out. Sweet and salty crashed a perfect blend on his tongue, like nectar from the long yellow flowers. A need to conquer, to spill his seed, to reign supreme above all others flooded his system from the top of his head and out through his tool.

It was done.

Today, the jungle would know that Jane belongs to him.

Tarzan thrust his hips forward and drove deep inside her welcoming body as the battle cry tore from his throat. "*Ahh-yahyahyah-yah-ahh!*"

Chapter Nine

*O*ne month later...

Jane sat under the shade of a tree, eating ripe fruit that had fallen. Warm sand on her bare ass, cool breeze on her face, and a newly weaved hula-type skirt around her waist. The vast and endless ocean spread before her this evening in a tablecloth of ever-changing swirls of blue.

A heaviness in her chest that had plagued her for the past few weeks seemed to intensify with every passing day.

Tarzan, bless his jungle heart, had tried everything to cheer her up, from introducing her to survival techniques to dressing up his constant gorilla companion in palm fronds and ivy. In turn, she'd taught him a few basic language skills. An adept student with a brilliant mind, he'd quickly learned many words.

The distractions helped for the moment. But when night fell and stars twinkled between the branches of their treetop nest, the ache of loneliness started anew.

She popped another berry into her mouth and bit down on the sun-ripened treat.

"Jane."

Glancing over her shoulder, a clean-shaven Tarzan strode out of the jungle. It's amazing what usable items would wash up on a beach. The muscles of his powerful legs cut through the deep sand as if the island were made of butter.

Oh...sweet, creamy butter on toast.

He stabbed the spear's round end into the sand and bent his knees to gracefully sit beside her. Worry creased between the dark brows of his handsome face. She'd been right in her assumption of the wonderful bone structure beneath his beard. However, they'd yet to tackle his headful of twig-encrusted dreadlocks.

"Jane..." He appeared to search his mind for a word. "Good?"

Jane sighed and leaned sideways to rest her head on his warm shoulder. "Yes, Tarzan. I'm fine."

"Jane not good. Jane sad."

Damn, can't pull the wool over this guy.

Lamb chops...with a lovely garlic-rosemary sauce.

"I'm fine, really." *Liar, liar, pants on fire.* She straightened and beamed her best fake smile. "See?"

Tarzan studied her for a moment, then turned away, shaking his head. "Jane sad. Tarzan bad."

Great, now she'd given a guilt complex to the island's only eligible human bachelor. She sighed again and rubbed a sandy hand, sticky with berry juice, over her forehead. As a provider, the wild guy rocked. As a lover, he blasted her off in a rocket to orbit planet Ecstasy every time.

So what the hell was her problem?

"It's not you. It's me." The cliché saying struck a funny bone, and she giggled toward her sandy toes.

Reaching around, he tugged a lock of hair at the back of her head, pulling harder until she looked up. Hope sparked in the rise of his brows. "*Ooh,*" he said softly.

"Yeah, I'm being silly. There isn't a woman in the world who wouldn't want to live in a tropical paradise with a gorgeous guy.

I mean, look at you." She cupped his cheek, the smooth, chiseled angle fitting perfectly in her sticky palm. "You're everything I ever dreamed of, and more."

Jane pulled her hand away, noting the streak of sandy, red juice she'd left behind. She should be a good jungle-mate and wash that off before the nighttime bugs that came out in droves discover a new feast.

Toward the ocean and its ceaseless waves, the sun sank lower and painted the sky a brilliant salmon color.

Cedar planked...

Tarzan dug his big feet into the sand and pushed to stand. He held out his hand. "Jane, come." His long fingers swallowed her hand as he easily pulled her upright. Linking fingers, he led her along the familiar path to the safety of the gorillas. Their approval hadn't been immediate, but over time, the band of apes grew to accept her.

Not as one of their own, but as Tarzan's mate.

Arriving at the base of the tree he'd chosen for their home, she noticed the trunk sported a new amenity: a vine that dangled from high above.

Tarzan released her fingers and placed nature's rope in her hand. "For Jane." He pushed one side of her bangs behind her ear, caressing her cheek as he drew away. "No fall."

Damn, what a guy. Warmth filled her cheeks and her eyes grew watery at his thoughtful, primitive gift. Ever since her debacle of swinging on the vine, she hadn't been comfortable alone in a tree. Nightmares plagued her, alternating between sinking yachts, pirates with rifles, and huge, ugly spiders—and Jane was sure she'd one day drop from the tree to her death.

But he was there. He was *always* there.

Her Tarzan.

Jane let go of the vine to stand on tiptoe and reach her arms around his strong neck. As natural as making love, his hands came around; one on her butt, the other at her back. He dipped his head and caught her lips, deepening the kiss with a swipe of his coconut-flavored tongue.

Kissing—another lesson her jungle man excelled at.

Heat curled within, and the heavy weight of homesickness tapered off. She leaned back to gaze into his eyes, smiling at the love that shone back.

"Whaddaya say we hit the branches, big boy?" Jane waggled her brows with meaning.

Tarzan's smile turned wolfish. "Fuck."

"Yeah," she said, chuckling. "We'll work on your language."

Behind them on the trail they'd just followed, a heavy thump hit the ground. A four-beat stride came fast. Jane turned to see Echo knuckle loping toward Tarzan.

"*Ooh-ooh!*" The gorilla's wide eyes sought them out.

Tarzan hunched down to exchange a flurry of hand and body language with his ape companion. With a sudden dark expression on his face, he turned toward her.

She immediately became alarmed.

Her mate pointed at the tree. "Jane. Tree."

"What about the tree?" She looked between the two males who remained in their crouched positions, studying the surrounding jungle.

"Up," he replied, the modulation of his no-nonsense voice quieter. "Bad *mans* come."

First survival rule of jungle life: Do as you're told and ask questions later.

Jane grabbed the newly installed vine and, with a little of Tarzan's help, she climbed to their sleeping nest. Only after he had seen that she'd made it to safety did he and Echo turn and disappear. Between giant ferns and wide-leafed plants, the pair moved as silently as the nighttime shadows.

Any number of bad men could have landed on the island. And what exactly made them *bad*? Maybe they were out fishing and decided to drop anchor for the night.

Maybe, she thoughtfully bit her lip, they were her ticket off the island.

But what about Tarzan? He cared for her deeply, as she cared for him. She might even, possibly, love him. When he left to hunt food, her heart missed him with every beat until a vine swung and he landed back home. How could she ever think of leaving him behind?

An echoing gunshot shattered the air.

Startled, Jane jumped into their bed of leaves. Her gaze darted over the edge of her and Tarzan's nest...and then all the jungle grew quiet.

Continue the adventures of Tarzan and Jane in *Forever My Jane*, Book 2 in the Jungle Island series!
Download here[1]

---

1. https://books2read.com/u/4DZg2O

Don't miss out!

Visit the website below and you can sign up to receive emails whenever Sheri Fredricks publishes a new book. There's no charge and no obligation.

https://books2read.com/r/B-A-WCJH-NHOW

BOOKS 2 READ

Connecting independent readers to independent writers.

Did you love *Lord of the Jungle*? Then you should read *Forever My Jane*[2] by Sheri Fredricks!

Forever My Jane

The Jungle Island Series, Book 2

On a calm morning out at sea, Jane is swept into a nightmare. Pirates sink her yacht and leave her for dead. Washed onto an uncharted island inhabited by a wild man with a hungry sexual curiosity, he claims her as his mate.

In the treetops, where life hinges on a diet of balance and steady nerves, the Lord of the Jungle—a powerful alpha male—rules his home. Through a language of grunts, she

---

understands his loneliness as the sole human living amongst a band of mountain gorillas. On her own, she's helpless, a captive without chains, and soon realizes the safest place on the island is next to his dominant side.

Tarzan's simple life took an unexpected turn when the female landed on his shores. His primitive need to mate is welcomed by her own desires for him. When the dreaded pirates return, so does the danger to his woman.

Jane will do anything to keep Tarzan alive, but in order to survive, she must trust his jungle instincts.

The steamy jungle just got hotter.

Read more at https://www.sherifredricks.com.

Also by Sheri Fredricks

Jungle Island
Lord of the Jungle
Forever My Jane
Jungle Love

The Centaurs
Remedy Maker
Portals of Oz
Troll-y Yours

The Facility
Esme, Door 1

The Rugged Series
Rugged Thirst

Standalone
Monica Beggs
Continuum

Watch for more at https://www.sherifredricks.com.

About the Author

Sheri Fredricks grew up on the central coast of California and resides within minutes of the pristine sunny beaches. She's a Border Collie fan, loves to eat sushi, and is addicted to Facebook. A writer of romance, she's the award-winning author of the shapeshifting Centaurs Series, Jungle Island Series, Monica Beggs, and many more. Sheri is currently writing more steamy, sexy stories for her voracious fans.

Read more at https://www.sherifredricks.com.